Meadow
and the Wise Ant

D.M.Gill

Illustrated by
Thushari Herath

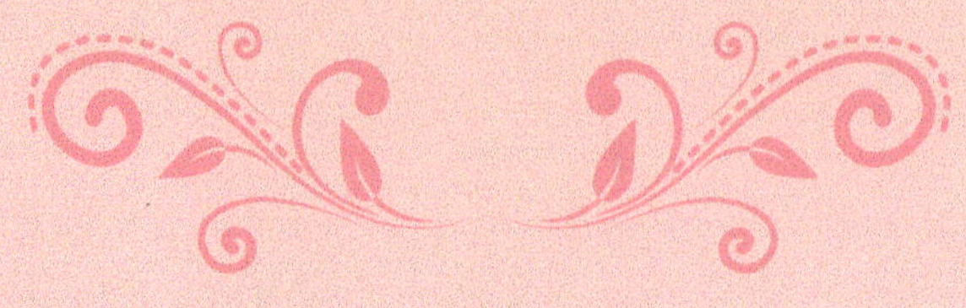

ISBN: 978-0-578-88010-5 (hardcover)
ISBN: 978-0-578-88009-9 (paperback)

This book belongs to:

On fluffy pink clouds, up in the sky,
is a magical place where children can fly.

They float on clouds and slide down rainbows.

They laugh and play,
making magic
wherever they go.

Up in these fluffy
pink clouds lived a
LITTLE GIRL
who loved to sing,
dance, cuddle and
twirl.

Meadow was her name,
and fashion was her game.

She mixed her hair clips,
so none looked the same.

She liked to be different because different is good.
Plus, when you lived up here,
no one was misunderstood.

Drawing is another thing that Meadow loved to do!
In her magical sketchbook,

flowers, stars and butterflies she drew.

But her biggest passion of all was to design,
but not just anything you may have in mind.

She wanted to make dresses out of
magical flowers and leaves
inspired by trees,

and tank tops tied with purple and pink ivy.

There were so many things
Meadow wanted to create,
but there was one
thing she believed
stood in the
way of her
fate.

If she wanted to be a designer,
she needed to sew.

and that was one thing
that she didn't know.

She gathered needles, thread and ribbon too,
then realized that sewing might
not be that easy to do.

The needles were too small,
the thread would split,
sewing was just so hard, and
Meadow decided to quit!

Frustrated and sad, she put away her
needles and thread.
Lying in bed, her designs danced around
in her head.

"Oh, how I wish with all of my heart,
that I knew how to sew, so I could share my art."

Meadow closed her eyes and as she lay sleeping
her wish flew through clouds and stars,
for help it was seeking.

Her wish traveled far,
looking for somewhere to land,
then it spotted the antenna
of a very wise Ant.

BING!

The Wise Ant's antenna started to ring.
He listened closely as Meadow's wish began to sing.
"What is that you say?" asked the very Wise Ant.
"There's a little girl in the clouds who needs my help?
She doesn't know how to sew. Well, neither do I.
But I'm old and wise,
so I can give her a little advice."

The Wise Ant pulled his legs close and started to
"ommm".

He traveled through the clouds and stars up to
Meadow's home.

THAT MORNING

when Meadow took a walk in the clouds,
she clearly heard a faint humming sound.

"Ommm," heard Meadow, so she began to look around.
"I think you'd see me better, young lady, if you sat down."

Meadow kneeled on the clouds and there was the Ant,
wearing shoes, a cape and a **purple top hat.**

"Who are you?" Meadow asked with curiosity.
"I'm just an ant, and last night your wish
came to visit me."
"My wish?" asked Meadow, feeling very confused.
"Yes, to make clothing with
*magical flowers and leaves
in different hues.*"

"That was my dream," said Meadow.
"But I've decided to quit,
I don't know how to sew.
It's too hard,
I simply can't do it."

Then tears fell from her eyes,
the Wise Ant could tell that
she was sad inside.

"Learning new things may be tough,
but you have to take time to learn
instead of giving up.

Believe in yourself
and you will succeed,
and most importantly,
never give up on your dream!"

Then the Wise Ant held out his palm,
and from it a magical flower grew.
"You see, I'm not only old and
wise, but I'm almost as
magical as you."

Meadow let out a giggle and said with a smile,
"Thank you for coming and
helping me find my style."

"Anytime," said the Wise Ant, and it wasn't long before, with a wink and nod, **he was gone.**

With her newfound confidence,
Meadow hurried back to work.
This time she used a sewing machine and
studied a sewing book.

Sewing straight was hard, but she tried and tried,
NO MATTER HOW LONG IT TOOK!

After practicing all week, Meadow knew it was time,
to open her magical sketchbook and
create one of her designs.

She measured her fabric, then she cut and she sewed,
just like the pages in her sewing book showed.
She picked magical flower petals and placed
each one on by hand.
Meadow was proud.

It was starting to
look grand!

And in another week's time,
she brought her first dress to life.
You should have seen the
sparkle in Meadow's big brown eyes!

Now she knew that she could do anything
she put her mind to,
and if you're reading this right now,
always believe that you can too!

E

Before you go,

Many times in our lives,
we count ourselves out
before we count ourselves in.
We believe that we'll fail,
before we believe that we'll win.
We already stop,
before we even begin.
But if we write our own stories
decide how it will end.
Then, I believe we'll find
the keys to the limitless
doorway within.

—love, d.m.gill

www.ingramcontent.com/pod-product-compliance
Lightning Source LLC
Chambersburg PA
CBHW041201100726
47911CB00016B/821